The Incident at Number 17 South Marlborough Street

James Kingston

A Story Shares book
Easy to read. Hard to put down.
storyshares.org

Storyshares

Storyshares, LLC

24 N. Bryn Mawr Avenue #340

Bryn Mawr, PA 19010-3304

www.storyshares.org

Inspiring reading with a new kind of book.

Interest Level: High School

Grade Level Equivalent: 1.7

9798885977548

Book design by Storyshares

Contents

Chapter One

I hear the noises in the street before I see what's happening. Loud sirens. Shouting.

I feel my heart beating faster in my chest. This is not good. I try to slow my breathing. I try to calm my mind. But I can't.

I struggle with the unexpected. I like routine. No, I need routine. But sometimes you have no control of what's happening in the world.

I move over to my bedroom window. It's only 7:30 AM. I haven't had my breakfast yet.

I'm dressed in my school uniform, and I've brushed my hair. The fringe is getting long now. Mum says I look cool. I'm not so sure.

Dad doesn't really mind about my hair. He notices the other things about me more. Like my routines.

Outside in the street, there are flashing blue lights. I can see two police cars and one ambulance. There are 15 people standing nearby. More people are standing on their doorsteps watching.

I can see Mr. Edwards, our next-door neighbour. He's waving his arms and talking to a paramedic. An ambulance driver.

I like the word paramedic. Para-medic. It feels nice to say. This paramedic looks like they don't want to talk to Mr. Edwards. They want to do their job.

The cars and police and paramedics are coming and going from Mrs. Warren's house.

Mrs. Warren is nice. She lives in the house next door to Mr. Edwards. Next door but one to us. Number 17 South Marlborough Street. We live at number 21.

Mrs. Warren is always kind and sometimes gives me 50p to buy sweets. I don't really like sweets, so I put the money in a glass jar on my windowsill.

I look at it now. I know that there are 78 50ps inside. I remember things like this. I know how much money that makes. £3.90.

I like sums. They always have a right answer.

I watch as the people move around outside. I look at my watch and it's nearly time for breakfast. I eat my breakfast at 7:45 AM every school day. I have two Weetabix and a banana. Separately

First, I pour the milk onto the Weetabix so that it's just enough to cover them. Then I eat the Weetabix. I cut each Weetabix into three pieces with my spoon.

I try to eat them as quickly as I can. They go soggy very fast. They're not nice when they're soggy. Once they are gone, I drink the milk with my spoon.

Then I peel my banana. Average-sized bananas take four bites. Smaller ones three bites. And some really big ones take five or even six bites. Sometimes there's a mushy black bit, usually at the bottom of the banana. This can spoil my breakfast.

I'm about to stop looking out of the window when I see two paramedics coming out of Mrs. Warren's house. They're carrying a stretcher with a sleeping bag on it. It's got something in it. It looks heavy.

The paramedics' faces look sad. Although, I can't really see clearly from here. Suddenly I get the feeling that something is wrong. What's in that bag?

It looks big enough and heavy enough to be a person. I know that they only put dead people in bags. They call them body bags. I saw it on a TV programme.

I want to move away from the window now. I feel scared. My heart's beating faster and I've got a lump in my throat. Like when I have to stand up and talk in class, but worse.

I like Mrs. Warren. She's kind. I hope she's not in the body bag. I hope she's not dead.

But she is old. She's at least 80. I remember my mum telling me. I remember her family coming for her eightieth birthday.

I watch the paramedics put the stretcher into the ambulance. Mr. Edwards makes a sign with his hands. He touches his head, then his chest twice. This is something to do with Jesus and God. I know because I've seen footballers do it after they score a goal. They thank God that the ball went into the net.

I don't know about God. The idea is scary.

One of the paramedics gets into the back of the ambulance with the body bag. The other one closes the door. I hear it bang. It sounds too loud.

The paramedic says something to Mr. Edwards. He shakes his head and moves away. The paramedic goes around to the other side of the ambulance, and I can't see him anymore.

There are fewer people in the street now. I count 12. There aren't as many people on their doorsteps, either.

The ambulance slowly moves away. Its lights are off and there's no siren. This means that it isn't an emergency anymore.

Chapter Two

Mum has put my breakfast out for me. A bowl. A spoon. The Weetabix box. A four-pint plastic carton of semi-skimmed milk (half full). And a banana.

She smiles at me when I come into the kitchen.

"Morning, Jay, did you sleep well?" she asks.

She always asks me this. Not long ago, I couldn't sleep. When I tried, I just felt more awake. This was when I first started high school.

I didn't like it at first. There were too many people. It was too loud. It's OK now. I have a routine. I'm better at sleeping now. I have a good routine.

I nod to my mum.

"What's happening outside?" I ask her.

She's thinking before answering, so I know that she's trying to think of the best thing to say. I know that she's going to tell me a lie. I don't like lies. They make life complicated.

People lie all the time. They tell you that they're OK when really they're sad. They tell you that they will come to your birthday party but really, they won't. They tell you that if you try hard, you'll do well at school, but not everyone can do well at school all the time.

"I think there's been a burglary," she says.

I'm surprised at this. I didn't expect her to say that. This isn't a lie.

"How do you know?" I ask her.

"Mr. Edwards came round earlier and told me," she says.

I think about this for a second. I didn't hear him. But I was in my bedroom with the radio on. I have a radio alarm clock. It wakes me at 7:00 AM on school days.

I listen to Chris Coombes on breakfast radio for 15 minutes, then I get up and get dressed. Chris Coombes is funny. He's loud, but he makes me laugh. He has the same first name as Dad.

"Was it Mrs. Warren's house that was burgled?" I ask my mum.

"Yes, it was, Jay," she answers.

"Is she dead?" I ask.

I watch Mum's face. It goes very pale.

"Why would you say that, James?"

Her voice is shaky and she's using my full name. That means that either she's shocked, angry, upset, or emotional in some way. I don't think she's angry with me.

"I saw the paramedics with a bag," I tell her.

I wait for her to say something, but she just stares through me.

"I think that Mrs. Warren was in the bag," I say. "The paramedics looked serious. And they didn't put on the lights or the sirens, so it wasn't an emergency. If she was dead, then it wouldn't be an emergency anymore."

Mum is very still. I can see her hands shaking slightly. I want to say something to make her feel better, but I don't know what.

"It's OK, Mum," I try. "I know that she was old. She's had a good, long life."

I say the words, but I don't mean them. I'm lying. It would have been true five minutes ago. But now that I know that Mrs. Warren's house was burgled, it's not true anymore.

Did the burglars kil her? I try not to think about it now.

Mum has sat down now. We have a small table in the corner of the kitchen. She's sitting opposite me. I can see her face, but her body is hidden by the Weetabix box.

I don't know what to do. I look at my watch and it's 7:50 AM. Usually I have eaten my breakfast by now. I should be brushing my teeth. Putting on my shoes. Getting ready to leave the house.

"Mum." I speak, but my voice seems quiet.

The house is quiet now, and feels bigger than normal. The clock is ticking very loudly.

"Mum." I try again.

I watch her face. She looks a bit better now. She's stopped shaking and is not as pale. She stops staring through me and looks into my eyes. Her eyes are wet. She nearly cried, but stopped herself. I think that she stopped herself for me.

"It's OK, Jay, you're right," she says. "Mrs. Warren was a lovely lady. And she had a long and happy life. I'm sure that…"

She doesn't finish her sentence. The words mumble away to nothing.

Mrs. Warren was a lovely lady. That's what she said. She was. Not Mrs. Warren is a lovely lady. She is not a lovely lady anymore. Because she is dead. Perhaps she has been killed.

We sit there looking at each other. I can hear the clock on the wall ticking. She doesn't know what to say. I don't know what to say. Suddenly, the doorbell rings. We both jump.

"Better eat your breakfast, Jay. I'll go and see who it is," she says.

Mum gets up and goes to answer the door.

I look at the Weetabix in my bowl. I don't feel hungry now. I feel like there's something in my stomach. It feels like air. It feels like air that's trying to escape.

I close my eyes and count in threes until I reach ninety. I think about Mrs. Warren. She was a lovely lady, but now she's not. She was a lovely lady. Yes, she was.

Chapter Three

I eat my breakfast. The pieces feel bigger than normal. They feel like they might stick in my throat. I drink more milk to stop this from happening.

It's a small banana today. Still, I eat it in five bites. Five small bites to make sure that I don't choke.

The door opens and my mum comes back in. She looks flustered. Like she doesn't know what to do.

A large policeman comes in behind her. He's very tall and looks very serious. He's holding his helmet like they do on TV programmes when someone's died.

"Hello, young man," he says to me.

I try to smile at him.

"What's your name?" he asks.

"James," I say.

Usually, I say my name is Jay. But this feels more formal. Like I should use my full name.

"Do you mind if I ask you a few questions, James?" He speaks in a kind way, but his words are hard. He's not lying, but he's very serious. He's trying to be casual, but I know he's not.

"OK," I say.

"Would you like a cup of tea or coffee, Mr...?" Mum asks.

"Oh, Robert is fine and no thank you, this won't take a minute," the man answers. "I suspect you have to get to school James. Do you go to Park Vale?"

"Yes," I answer.

"A good school. My son used to go there, but he's 20 now. Been in the army for two years. Stationed out in Germany at the moment," Robert says.

I wonder why he's telling me this.

"OK, James," he says.

He looks at my eyes all the time. It makes me feel a mixture of uncomfortable and calm. I don't know if I like him. I don't know if he's a good person. I think that he can be a very strong person. Perhaps a violent person.

He takes out a notebook.

"Have you noticed anything out of the ordinary lately in your street?" he asks.

I think about this for a minute.

I notice when things are different. I have my routine. I eat the same things for breakfast every day. I leave the house to go to school at the same time every day. *But not today,* I think, glancing at the clock.

I walk the same way to Dave's house. I cross the road at the traffic lights on the corner of Park Vale Drive. We walk past the sycamore tree outside Olivia Jones' house.

Olivia Jones is nice. She always says "Hey" to me. She's got dark brown hair and a pretty face. She has very red lips and very white skin. She seems sad. I don't know why. I'd like to ask her but I find it hard to speak to girls, except for Mum.

"James," my mother prompts me. She knows that I'm thinking about any unusual things I've noticed, but Robert is getting restless.

I can't think of anything out of the ordinary. It's strange, because usually I notice everything. Today, though, I feel dazed. I shake my head.

"Sorry," Mum says. "We're both a bit shocked by it all. This is such a quiet street and all the neighbours really look out for each other. I think he's still processing what's happened."

Robert nods his head and slowly gets up. He looks like he's thinking. He takes a card from his pocket and hands it to Mum.

"If you do think of anything, Mrs. Allen. And you, James. You can call me on this number. Any time, any day. OK?" he says.

I smile and nod. Mum follows him out of the kitchen.

I'm about to get up and call him back. I have thought of something out of the ordinary. Something very out of the ordinary.

A white van parked outside Dave's house. It was last Tuesday. It was there every day. For three days. It's not usually there. I know all the cars in our street. And their numberplates.

Ours is a grey Mondeo KL54 DTF. Dave's family have a white Vauxhall Zafira BP12 TFR. He calls it a people carrier. This makes me laugh. The car has extra seats in the back.

Dave has three little sisters. Two of them are identical twins. I can't tell which one is which. Dave says that Lucy has a dimple on her left cheek and Amy is 3mm taller than Lucy. I haven't noticed these things.

The van was white. It was a Ford Transit LT56 YTJ. It was there last Tuesday. And Wednesday. And Thursday. It was gone on Friday.

Dave said it was plumbers. They were working at the empty house opposite Dave.

That house is rented and people move in and out a lot. Our house and Dave's are owned by a mortgage company. Our families pay them money so that we can live there. One day, we will own the house and stop paying the mortgage.

"Not unless we die first," Dad says, and Mum tells him not to joke around.

I don't understand that joke. Is dying supposed to be funny?

I hear Mum shut the door and I think about the plumber's van. It was out of the ordinary. I want to tell Mum, but there's no time.

"Are you still sitting there, Jay? You'll be late for school," Mum says when she comes back in. Then she adds, "Sorry, Jay, I didn't mean it like that. Are you OK?"

I nod.

"I'm fine, Mum," I say.

I get up and go over to her. She hugs me, and I hug her back.

"I love you, Jay. I know that this has been a horrible shock. We can talk more after school if you want," Mum says.

"That'd be good, Mum, thanks," I say.

She kisses me on the cheek and I go out of the kitchen.

Chapter Four

I like our bathroom. It's a calm place. I like that there are nine tiles across the wall and nine tiles up the wall. I know that nine times nine is 81. So there are 81 tiles.

I love multiples of nine. I also love multiples of three. I don't know why. They make me feel calmer. It's part of my routine.

I used to count everything. I used to put everything neatly in rows of threes and nines. Sixes or fives if I couldn't use threes or nines.

A doctor told me that I needed to stop doing it. Sometimes I used to count out loud. People would look at me. It was embarrassing for Mum.

I count in my head now. The doctor doesn't know. My mum says I'm doing well and pretends she doesn't know that I count things in my head. I think she knows.

It takes 187 steps to get to Dave's house. There are thirteen steps in my house. I walk up the stairs in nine steps and count seven as two steps, because the word seven has two syllables. I also add three "ands" so that I count nine steps.

I floss my teeth every day. I push the floss between my teeth and rub. I don't count this. The bathroom is calm, so I don't need to count. I floss the top teeth first. The dentist says it's important to floss.

The dentist has very hairy arms. We used to have a female dentist called Emily. She was nice. She filled my tooth and was careful with the injection.

I don't think the dentist we have now would be careful. I don't want him to inject my gums, so I floss and brush carefully every day. It's part of my routine.

The dentist pokes metal spikes into my gums and makes them bleed. Then he says, "Good work, Jimbo." He's the only person who calls me this. I don't like it but he's big and scary, so I just smile.

The dental nurse is kind and gives me a sticker. I feel too old for stickers now. I am nearly fourteen.

After I floss, I brush my teeth. I use Colgate. It's very minty and makes my mouth feel fresh. I brush up and down on the front of my teeth. Then I do the tops. Then the inside.

I spit and rinse three times during brushes. Sometimes the water is pink because of my blood. Today it's clear. This is a good thing. It means that I don't have gum disease.

Gum disease is not good. It can make your teeth fall out. If you don't brush your teeth you can die. The disease can go to your brain. I saw a TV programme about it.

When I've brushed my teeth I use the toilet, then wash my hands. I go back downstairs.

Today, Mum has put my packed lunch in my schoolbag. Usually, I take it out of the fridge myself. I'm later today because of the incident. An incident is something that happens. Usually something bad.

I have a sandwich for lunch. Usually ham or cheese. Or ham and cheese. I like ham. I like cheese. Sometimes at Christmas Mum buys different cheese. I tried it once. It wasn't nice.

With my sandwich, I have a bottle of orange squash. Sometimes I have apple and blackcurrant. Sometimes I just have water.

I have some fruit. Grapes, an apple, an orange, a satsuma or clementine, a plum, a pear. I love fruit. It's fresh and tastes healthy.

I also have a packet of crisps. Beef or bacon are my favourite flavours, but I like all crisps. I also have a small chocolate bar.

I put on my coat and pull on my bag. I can feel Mum watching me.

She doesn't usually watch me. She is concerned. She knows about my routine. She doesn't want me to get upset. She comes and hugs me again.

"See you tonight, then. Hope you have a good day," she says.

"Thanks, Mum, you too," I say.

She kisses me on the cheek again and I leave the house.

It's cold outside. I put my hands deep into my coat pockets. One police car is still outside Mrs. Warren's house. There is yellow tape around the driveway. It flutters in the breeze.

I think about Mrs. Warren. It makes me sad. She was nice. *She had a good life,* I tell myself. She had a happy and long life.

I try to imagine being 80. I can't really do it. It feels strange. I wonder if I'll still have a routine when I'm older.

The doctor told me that adults can have routines. He told me that they need to control their urges. He told me that I'm neurologically diverse. It's difficult to say. It means that my brain works in a different way to most people.

I like routine. It helps me stay calm.

The doctor told me that it's important not to count. He told me that I have OCD. It means obsessive compulsive disorder.

He tried to give me tablets to cure me. They made me feel sick. Mum and Dad threw them away. I don't see the doctor anymore. I count in my head, and that's OK.

It takes 187 steps to get to Dave's house. When I get there, Dave is standing on his doorstep. Usually, he's not ready and I wait in his house while he finishes getting ready.

"What time do you call this, Jay?" Dave says, looking at his watch.

I know he's joking. Dave is never serious. He's very calm. I like Dave.

"There was an incident," I say.

"Yeah, I saw the old bill go past," he says.

Dave likes using slang words. He says old bill instead of police. He says noggin instead of head.

"What's going on in your noggin, eh, Jay?" he sometimes asks me.

Dave is nice. I like Dave. He's bigger than me. He's very strong. But he doesn't fight like some of the boys. I don't like fighting.

Carl Tate tried to fight with me once. I had to hold onto him tightly until he stopped trying to fight me. After that, the headmaster called my parents. They had to come to school and talk to Carl Tate's parents. Carl doesn't try to fight me anymore. Nobody does.

We start walking down our street. It's called South Marlborough Street. Marlborough is somewhere in London.

London is a long way away. I went there once on the train with Mum and Dad. It was very loud and smelly. I didn't like it.

There is no North Marlborough Street. Or East. Or West. I don't know why.

"So what was happening, Jay?" Dave asks. "Give us the goss."

Goss is short for gossip. Gossip is talking about things that you shouldn't talk about.

I move closer to Dave.

"Someone burgled Mrs. Warren's house," I tell him.

Dave's eyes go wide and he gasps.

"Dave, I think they killed her," I say.

Dave is silent for a minute. He liked Mrs. Warren, too. She gave him 50p and he did spend it on sweets. Dave likes sweets. He often has toothache.

"I can't believe it, Jay," he says. "Who would do something like that? She was just a kind old lady. Have they caught the burglars?"

"No, I don't think so," I say. "A policeman came to my house and asked me if I'd seen anything out of the ordinary."

"Geez, out of the ordinary, what's that supposed to mean?" he asks.

"Something different, like that van last week. The plumbers," I remind him.

"Hmmm," says Dave.

He's thinking now. I can tell that he has an idea. Dave has good ideas.

He invented the acrobat game. We play it at break and lunch break in school. We play it on the grass. We can't do it now, because it's November and the grass is out of bounds. Out of bounds means that it's too wet and muddy.

Dave made the acrobat game because of Gilly. Gilly is my other friend. Gilly is short for Gilbert. Gilly is small and quick. He's funny and can make all the class laugh. The teachers pretend that they don't like him. They shout at him but I can see that they like him, really.

Gilly can walk on his hands. He can do somersaults and cartwheels. In the acrobat game, Gilly walks on his hands and we have to try to copy him.

Dave and I can't walk on our hands. It's very hard. I don't know how Gilly can do it.

"Do you know what, Jay? I think you might be onto something," Dave says.

"What, Dave? What do you think?" I ask.

"Those plumbers," he says. "I heard my dad talking to Jeff next door."

Jeff is a builder. He's strong and scary. He can lift big pieces of wood and concrete. I'm not sure if I like Jeff.

I like Dave's dad. Dave's dad is big and strong like Dave. He's strong in a different way to Jeff, though.

Jeff is stronger, I think. His muscles bulge and he's thin. He's moves smoothly. I think he was good at sport when he was younger.

Dave's family are from Nigeria. Nigeria is in Africa. Dave was born in St. Michael's hospital in Bristol, like me. He's English. He's Black, but he's still English.

There are seven Black people in my class. There are 12 white people, including me. There are 11 Asian people. The Asian people are mostly from the Philippines.

It's good to have different people in my class. I like learning about their cultures.

Some of the Asian girls wear head scarves. I like these. They make their faces look pretty. Like they're in a picture frame.

Mum told me that I can't say that. She said people would think I was racist. This doesn't make any sense. I don't understand why people are racist. I like people that are nice. Colour doesn't matter.

Except for bananas. I don't like black bananas. They're too mushy. I don't like green bananas either. They're too hard and difficult to peel. Yellow bananas are best.

"What were they saying, Dave?" I ask.

"They were saying that those bloody plumbers are a bunch of wrong uns," he says

A wrong un is a bad person. It means wrong one. Like you chose the wrong one. Bad luck. You lose.

I don't like slang. Although, it can be funny when Dave says it.

Dave is serious now. He's not usually serious. He liked Mrs. Warren.

"Yeah. I remember now. They said that they were taking far too long in that house," he says "Jeff had done some work there for the last tenants. He said there was no way that there was enough work in there to last them that long. He said they must be scammers."

I'm not sure what a scammer is, but I don't say. It sounds bad.

"What do you want to do, then, Dave? Should we call the police?" I ask.

"Need to find out a bit more first, mate. Hey, look, there's Liv," Dave says.

Liv is what everyone calls Olivia. I like it. I like it when people shorten their names.

Liv waves to us and we both wave back.

"Morning, Liv," Dave calls. Dave likes Liv, too.

She looks sad today. Liv is very good at the guitar. I heard her playing it once. Her fingers moved so quickly and accurately. It sounded sad and happy at the same time.

Sometimes Dad plays the guitar. He's not as fast or accurate as Liv. I do like it, though. Dad tried to show me how to do it, but I couldn't do it. I like listening to music. That's all.

I can see the school gates up ahead. It's getting louder now. There are lots of children around. I stay close to Dave. These are the worst parts of school. The bits where everyone is moving around at the same time.

Dave turns to me as we stop to cross the road.

"Look, mate, I think I've got a plan. Just need to speak to Gilly first." He winks at me. He seems happy with his idea. "Let's talk about it at break, yeah?"

The traffic lights go red and the green man appears. The beeping starts and we cross the road.

Now we're in the middle of all the students. They are lots of different sizes. It smells like mint and cereal. I think that some people brush their teeth better than others.

I can see Liv walking ahead of us. She's on her own. She often is. I want to talk to Liv, but I don't know how.

Suddenly, Dave and I jerk forward. We turn around together and Gilly appears out of nowhere.

He slaps us both on our backs. "Morning, fellas," he says.

Gilly likes slang, too. A fella is a person. Usually a boy or a man. So is a chap or a geezer. Girls can be chicks or birds, but these aren't nice things to say.

"What's going on with you two today, eh?" says Gilly. "What's with the long faces? You look like someone just died."

Chapter Five

At break time, I stand on my own in the playground. There are crowds of children. Some stand talking. Some run around. Some kick a football against the wall. It is very loud.

I'm cold, so I rub my hands together. I see Dave and Gilly. They're walking toward me. Dave is speaking very quickly. Gilly is moving his hands around. So is Dave.

"All right, Jay?" Dave asks.

Gilly punches me on the shoulder and smiles. It hurts a tiny bit, but I don't mind. Gilly likes to touch people. He is very physical. That's what Mr. Davis said.

Mr. Davis is nice. He has no hair. The top of his head is shiny. I've heard the older children call him Mr. Eavis.

Mr. Eavis is a farmer. They think Mr. Davis looks like Mr. Eavis. I've never seen Mr. Eavis, so I don't know if it's true.

Mr. Eavis has a farm in Glastonbury. Every summer, he lets people sleep in his fields and listen to music. I saw it once on the TV. There were lots of crowds. It didn't look good.

"We've got a plan, Jay," says Dave.

"You're gonna love this, Jay mate," says Gilly.

"What's the plan?" I ask.

"Do you remember when we were playing footy in the street the other day, and the ball went over into the back garden of that empty house?" asks Dave.

I do remember. Sometimes we play football in the street. It's a quiet street, so it's safe.

It's not safe anymore. There are burglars there that might be murderers. A murderer is someone who kills someone else.

I hope that the burglars didn't murder Mrs. Warren. I hope she died naturally, and it was just a coincidence. A coincidence is when two things happen at the same time, but not because of each other. This is quite a confusing idea.

"Yes, I remember," I say.

"Well, you went in for your tea after that but I went and climbed over the gate to get the ball back," Dave says. "It was quite overgrown in the back garden. I got stung to bits by nettles and scratched to pieces trying to find that ball. But I got it in the end. And do you know what, Jay?"

"No," I say.

"While I was in there, I'm sure I noticed that the upstairs window was open. I only remember because I heard something move. When I looked up, this big magpie had just flown off and I saw the open window. And I remember thinking, that's strange, that shouldn't have been left open," Dave says.

"So what's the plan, then?" I ask. I think I know what the plan is, but I don't like it.

"That's where I come in," says Gilly proudly.

"There's a big old sycamore tree in the back garden," says Dave. "And I reckon that Gilly could easily shin up the trunk and climb in through the window. Have a look around. See if he can find any clues about these plumbers "

"I know I can," says Gilly. "You show me a tree and I can climb it. You show me an open window and I'll climb up and get in."

I don't know if this is true.

Gilly is good at climbing trees. Gilly is from the countryside. He used to live on a farm. When his dad died, his mum had to sell the farm.

Sometimes Gilly is sad about his dad. He also had a brother who got killed in the army. His brother was called Scott. Gilly doesn't talk about Scott much.

Once he told us that Scott was the champion of the Cooper's Hill Cheese Race. Gilly did the race when he was nine. Lots of mad people chase a round of cheese down a steep hill in Gloucestershire. Gilly says it's a Pagan tradition. I don't know what Pagan means. It sounds scary.

"This is breaking into someone's house," I say. "It's illegal."

"It's not breaking in if the window's open," says Dave.

"It's still illegal," I say.

"Maybe it is," says Gilly. "But you want to find out who killed Mrs. Warren, don't you?"

Gilly liked Mrs. Warren, too. Everyone liked Mrs. Warren. Except for Mr. Edwards. Mr. Edwards doesn't like anyone. Mum says he's a grumpy old codger.

A codger is slang for someone old. This is a slang word I like. It sounds right.

I do want to find out who killed Mrs. Warren, so I nod my head.

"All right, then," says Gilly. "I'll come to yours tonight after tea, Dave. Jay, are you gonna meet us there, too? We'll need a lookout."

I nod. I don't want to do it, but I want to help to find the burglars. And I like the way Gilly says all right. He has a strong accent. It sounds like alroit. He says 'I' like 'oy'.

Some people call him a bumpkin. This means he's from the countryside. Gilly doesn't mind. He loves the countryside.

He says that when he's older, he's going to buy back the farm. Then he's going to have the best flock of sheep in all of Gloucestershire. They'll graze on Cooper's Hill and have the softest fleeces in the country.

I like Gilly. I hope he does buy the farm. He doesn't like the city. Sometimes he picks a piece of grass and puts it in his mouth. The end sticks out like a cigarette.

When I asked him what he was doing, he just said, "Chewing the cud, Jay."

Chewing the cud is what cows do. Maybe farmers have to do it too, to teach the cows how to eat.

When I get home, Mum's in the kitchen. She's chopping up vegetables. We're having Spaghetti Bolognese.

I like pasta. I like tomato sauce. I like most food.

Mum is happy. She has the radio on and she's humming to a song.

"Hi, Jay, how was your day?" she asks.

"It was OK, thanks. How was yours?" I ask.

"I spoke to Mr. Edwards again," she says.

I wait for her to continue.

"He went to the hospital to find out about Mrs. Warren. Her family were there," she says. "Mr. Edwards has known the Warrens for a long time. They told him that she had died peacefully in her sleep. She wasn't killed by the burglars. She didn't die from a heart attack when she saw them in her house. She was already dead when they broke into her home."

I think about this. This is good. The burglars aren't murderers. They're just burglars.

I want this to make me feel better. But it doesn't. I'm nervous about tonight.

"Are you OK, Jay?" Mum asks. "This is good news. Mrs. Warren passed away naturally. Like we said, she had a long and happy life and passed away peacefully in her sleep. It was just coincidence that her house was burgled."

I don't understand how they know that she died peacefully in her sleep. She might have woken up and died painfully. I want to say this, but I don't.

I also don't like the coincidence again. This makes me feel anxious, so I focus on the tiles around the kitchen sink. I count 14 across. I already know there are 14 tiles across. While I do this, I straighten the placemats on the counter.

"Are you hungry, Jay?" Mum asks.

"A bit," I say.

"Dad will be home soon," she says. "Have you got any homework to do tonight?"

"No, mum. I said I'd go round to Dave's after tea. Is that OK?" I ask.

"That's fine, love," she says.

Mum likes Dave. Mum and Dad are friends with Dave's parents. Dave's dad is an architect. My dad is a writer. He writes about building materials.

When Dave's parents come round for tea, they talk about buildings. I don't understand lots of the words. Like brutalist and modernist. Dad tells me they're styles of buildings.

Dave's dad is very clever. He designed the new town hall. The old town hall wasn't safe. The new town hall doesn't look as nice as the old one. I don't say this to Dave or his dad.

Dave's parents are from Nigeria. They came here because Dave's dad wanted to work. In Nigeria, there isn't enough work for him. Dave's dad says that Nigeria is corrupt. Dad says the UK is corrupt, and they laugh.

I don't really understand what corrupt means. Dad says it's when leaders take money they shouldn't.

Dad's family are Welsh. Wales is a small country next to England. When we visit *Nain* and *Taid,* we go over a long bridge. *Nain* and *Taid* means Nana and Grandad in Welsh.

Nain and *Taid* speak Welsh together. It sounds nice. I don't understand any of the words. Sometimes they teach me some words.

Pam means who. *Araf* means slow. *Pont* means bridge. These are some of the Welsh words I remember.

Mum's family are English. They are from the North. It takes a long time to get there. When we visit Mum's family, I sleep in the car.

It rains a lot in the North and it's cold. All the people speak in a funny accent. I like accents. I think I like *Nain* and *Taid's* accent the best. It sounds like singing. I also like Gilly's accent.

I hear the door open. Dad's home. Dad leaves to go to work before I get up. He works in an office in Bristol. He uses a computer and writes information for websites.

I tried to read some of Dad's work. There were lots of long words like fenestration, this is about windows. And aluminium extrusion, this is about metal.

Dad comes into the kitchen and kisses Mum on the lips. Mum is happier now. She loves Dad. Dad loves Mum, too, but it's not as easy to see. Dad comes over to me and gives me a hug.

"How are you both?" he asks.

"Good," I say.

"Mum messaged me about what happened this morning," he says.

Dad had already gone to work when the police and ambulance arrived.

"Are you sure you're OK, Jay?" he asks. "I know how much you liked Mrs. Warren."

"I'm fine, dad," I say.

"Mr. Edwards went to see the family today, Chris. She died in her sleep. It was nothing to do with the break-in," Mum says. She looks at me and says, "That's good, isn't it, Jay?"

She wants to make me feel better, but it doesn't work.

"How was work, Dad?" I ask. I don't want to talk about Mrs. Warren or death or burglars anymore.

"Same old, same old, Jay. Those websites won't write themselves," Dad says.

This is a joke, so I smile. I don't find it funny, though. Of course websites can't write themselves.

Sometimes Dad says that I'm too straightforward. I don't see the subtleties of language. I can see that there's a b in subtleties, but I don't know why it's there.

Dad says I see things in black and white. This is wrong. I see all sorts of colours. This is me being too straightforward.

"What's for tea, Em?" Dad asks.

Mum's name is Emily. Dad calls her Em.

"Spag bol," Mum says.

Spag bol is short for Spaghetti Bolognese. I like shortening names. Spag bol is Italian.

When I was younger, we went to Italy on a plane. I don't remember much about it. I remember it being hot. I remember the cars driving very fast. The people smiled a lot. There were lots of children in restaurants. I think I liked it.

After we've eaten our tea, I get ready to go to Dave's house. I put on my coat and hat. I say goodbye to Mum and Dad. I tell them I'll be back by 8:30.

Chapter Six

It's cold and dark outside. The streetlights are orange. They make everything look different.

I like the night. I look up at the sky. The stars are shining, and the moon is almost full.

I like space. I like the idea of how big it is. It makes everything else feel very small.

Dad told me that when you look at the stars, you're looking into the past. This is because the light takes millions of years to reach our eyes. The stars we can see aren't there anymore. Lots of them have died or become black holes.

Dad says that black holes might be passages to other universes. He says that some scientists believe there are an infinite number of universes. And in these universes, there are different versions of me and him and Mum and Dave and Gilly. And all the other people doing all the different possible things we could ever do.

When he told me this, I thought it was a joke. But it's not. He was serious.

When I get near to Dave's house, I can see him and Gilly waiting for me in the street. I walk up to them and Dave taps his watch like he did this morning.

The morning feels like a long time ago. More has happened today than on most days. It feels like a long day. Like the holidays, or Christmas Day.

I like Christmas. People are happier. They smile at me and say "Merry Christmas." I smile back and say "Merry Christmas" to them.

"All right, Jay mate," says Dave. "You up for this?"

Gilly laughs. "Of course he's up for it. He's the brains behind the mission."

"It wasn't my idea,' I say.

"Never mind that," says Dave. "Let's go and have a look at that window to see if Gilly can get up there."

Gilly cracks his fingers. "If there's an open window and a sturdy drainpipe, I can get up there " he says.

We cross the road to the empty house. The other houses in the street have lights on inside. This one is dark. We look around to make sure no one is watching us. We walk down the drive.

The houses in South Marlborough Street are all joined together. This is called a terrace. Dad says they were built by the Victorians.

The Victorians lived in Britain in the 19th century. They built lots of houses for working people. They were called Victorians because of Queen Victoria.

The queen today is Queen Elizabeth, but we aren't called Elizabethans. That's because she's Elizabeth the Second. Elizabethans lived a long time ago. Before the Victorians. That was when Elizabeth the First was queen.

We sometimes learn about kings and queens in history. It's quite boring. Some parts are interesting. But there are lots of dates and names that sound alike.

The front garden is small, ike ours. There are lots of nettles and weeds. There is a small wall. It separates the path from next door. At the bottom of the path is a wooden gate. It is painted white.

Gilly jumps onto the wall and then onto the gate. He drops down on the other side before we move.

"Do you want to go next?" asks Dave.

"Didn't you want me to keep a lookout?" I ask.

"No need, really," says Dave.

I climb onto the wall. It's not very high. It's not even as tall as me, but it feels taller. I lean over and pull myself onto the top of the gate. I lift one leg over and sit astride the gate.

I lift the other one over and lower myself down, holding on with both hands. I let myself drop and am surprised that the ground is so close. Gilly smiles at me and takes out a torch from his coat pocket.

He switches it on and presses it against the bottom of his jaw. The bottom half of his face lights up and I want to laugh. Then Dave drops down onto the floor next to me and knocks me forward into Gilly. We all laugh, then stop ourselves.

Dave speaks quietly. "Shine the torch up at the house, Gil."

Gilly shines the torch up. Dave was right. One of the back bedroom windows is open.

The houses on South Marlborough Street have sash windows. They slide wide open and you can easily climb through. I climbed through our kitchen window once when I came home from school. Mum was out and it was before I had a key.

"Did you see it, fellas?" asks Dave.

We both nod.

"What about that tree, Gilly? Shine your torch over that way a minute." Dave waves his arm toward a large sycamore tree.

Its branches reach out close to the house. I can see that one big branch goes close to the window. I wouldn't want to climb along it, but I can tell that Gil y does. Gilly smiles.

"Hold this, Dave," Gilly says. "And shine it at the trunk. Try to keep it just above me as I climb."

Dave takes the torch from Gilly. He shines it at the tree. There are no low branches. I know that Dave and I could never climb that tree.

The trunk at the bottom is very wide. It must be at least three metres circumference. We learn about circumference in maths. I like formulas. They help you to understand the world.

Gilly walks slowly to the tree. Dave shines the light on the trunk just above Gilly's head. Gilly reaches the tree. He pats the trunk. Then he puts his arms round it. It looks like he's hugging the tree.

Dad says that some people are called tree huggers. They want to save the planet. Dad says they have good intentions, but go about things the wrong way.

Gilly starts moving up the tree. I don't know how he does it. It looks like he's stuck to the tree. It looks like his hands must have glue on them or Velcro or some sort of grips. He pulls himself onto the lowest branch.

From there, he stands up and grabs a branch above his head. He pulls himself up onto the branch he's holding, then does the same onto a higher branch Soon, he's on the branch that goes near to the open window.

Gilly stops for a second. He moves his legs slightly and the branch he's standing on shakes. A few leaves fall to the ground, and a few of the seeds. Helicopters. They are called this because they spin when they fall.

Gilly slowly walks along the branch. He holds onto different branches above him that look very thin. Dave keeps moving the torch in front of Gilly. Gilly reaches the end of the branch. I can see it bending under his weight.

I hope it doesn't snap. Gilly would be hurt if he fell from there. He is quite high up. I think about eight metres.

Gilly stands still. I start counting in ones. He stands still for about 30 seconds. Then he lets himself fall forward and his hands touch the wall of the house. He's leaning on the outside of the house now.

He crouches down and reaches for the open window. Dave shines the torch on the window, and we can see Gilly's fingers. He's trying to reach the open part of the window. Suddenly, he gets it.

The branch stops moving. Gilly pulls. The window moves upward. He looks around. Then he dives through the open window headfirst.

It looks impossible. There is no sound when he enters the house.

Gilly's face appears at the window. He shields his eyes against the light of the torch.

"Dave, Jay. I'm gonna try and get downstairs," he says. "It's really dark in here, obviously. I'll try not to knock anything over. If there is anything in here to knock over. Wait there, and if I can, I'll come and open the back door to let you in."

I stand with Dave in the garden. It's very cold. It's also dark. Time feels like it's going slowly. We don't speak. We just wait.

I can hear traffic noises. They're not from South Marlborough Street. The noise comes from further away. We wait. I rub my hands together to keep warm.

Gilly's taking a long time. Perhaps he's lost in the house. Perhaps he's trapped.

Suddenly, we see Gilly's face behind the frosted glass of the back door. I can hear him trying to open the door. It doesn't move. Then it slowly opens inwards.

"Jay, Dave," says Gilly, in a quiet but obviously excited voice. "You've gotta see it n here. It's so weird. And it stinks."

"What is it, Gil?" I ask.

"Pass me the torch, Dave, and follow me," he says.

Dave gives Gilly the torch and we follow him into the house. I can't see much in the house. We walk slowly so we don't bump into anything.

Gilly leads us through the kitchen and into the hall. The house has the same layout as mine and Dave's. It feels strange to be in there. I want to get out, but I also want to follow Gilly.

He leads us up the stairs. At the top of the stairs there's a landing, like in our house. Three bedroom doors are all closed. In this house, there's another staircase that goes up into the loft.

Gilly turns round.

"Up here, fellas. Can you smell it yet?" he asks.

We follow Gilly up the extra stairs. At the top, there's a small landing. There are two closed doors. Gilly opens the left one.

When we go inside, it's like going into a strange dream. There's a dull humming sound. There's low light coming from the floor. And there are tall plants everywhere. The plants smell very strongly.

I know that they are weed plants. Weed is a drug. We learnt about it in school. Why are there weed plants in this house's loft?

"It's weed," says Gilly. "And loads of it."

Dave shines the torch around the room.

"I think we should probably get out of here," says Dave.

I nod, although they can't see me do it. I don't like it in here. The smell is too strong. The plants are too big. They make strange shadows on the floor and the walls.

Suddenly, the room seems brighter. I can see Gilly's and Dave's faces. They look scared.

"What was that?" asks Gilly.

Dave puts his finger to his lips.

"Shhh," he whispers. "I think there's someone in the house."

He's right. The light has gone on downstairs. I can hear movement. I can hear what sounds like voices.

"Oh no, they're coming up here," says Gilly. "Quick, hide."

It all happens so quickly. I'm not sure which order is right. I'm kneeling on the floor behind one of the weed plants. I feel sick because of the smell.

I can see Dave's foot sticking out from behind another plant. I want to tell him I can see it. To warn him. But the people are coming up here now. I can hear their footsteps on the stairs.

I can hear their voices. I can't hear what they're saying. I think I recognize one of the voices. Yes. It sounds familiar. But I don't know where from.

The men come into the room. The light has changed. It's darker because of their shadows. They move slowly through the weed plants.

I hold my breath. Then I see quick movement. Gilly's running out of the room. I turn to look for Dave, but he's racing after Gilly.

I don't know what to do. I'm not as fast as Dave or Gilly.

One of the men runs after Dave and Gilly. Then I feel a hand on my shoulder. The other man has found me. I can't move.

He grips my shoulders tight. He feels very strong. He smells of sweat. It mixes with the smell of the weed plants and makes me feel sick.

In one movement, the man picks me up and puts me over his shoulder. He doesn't say anything. I think I know this man. But it's too dark to see. He carries me out of the room.

Then the other man is back. They speak in low voices.

"Little gits were too quick."

"Damn it, Si. What are we gonna do with this one?"

They're talking about me. I'm "this one."

I'm glad that Dave and Gilly have escaped. I hope they go and phone the police. Or get our parents. I'm scared now.

"I think we need to do this officially," the man who's holding me says. Then he puts me down.

I look up at him and I'm shocked. It's Robert. The policeman who came to our house. He smiles at me.

"You're under arrest, little fella," he says. He turns me around and places handcuffs round my wrists. The metal feels cold, and he closes them too tight. "For breaking and entering. Simon, take him down to the car."

Simon holds my shoulders. We walk through the house together. I want to escape. I want to run.

Something seems very wrong. Policemen don't pick people up

like that. It wasn't right.

Simon puts me in the back of the police car and gets in next to me. Robert gets in the front. He turns round and nods to Simon.

I look at Simon. I think I recognise him, too. Maybe he was the policeman at Mrs. Warren's house this morning. I don't think so, though. I think I've seen him somewhere else.

"Sorted," Robert says to Simon. Then he looks at me. "Let's get you down to the station, then, lad. I think you've got some explaining to do."

Chapter Seven

The car moves away slowly. I feel scared. Robert and Simon are strange. Policemen are supposed to help. I don't think they want to help.

Simon leans forward and speaks to Robert. I can't hear what they say. Robert drives slowly.

"OK, James, this is how it is. You're a good lad, aren't you? From a good family. You don't want this on your record, do you?" asks Robert.

I don't know what he means. I shake my head.

"Good lad," he says. "Now, that house you were in. Well, we've been watching that place for a while. Haven't we, Simon?"

"Yes, we have," says Simon. "It's an undercover operation."

Simon laughs after he says this. I don't like Simon. I don't like Robert, either.

I notice that the police car is not going in the right direction. The police station is the other way.

"Let me tell you what's going to happen now," says Robert.

I wait for him to continue.

"We're going to take you back to your street," he says. "You're going to find those friends of yours. And you're going to tell them what Simon told you. You know the game, Simon Says?"

I nod.

"Well," says Robert, and Simon starts to speak.

"Simon says that you're to tell your friends to keep quiet about what they saw in that house," he says. "You're going to tell them that the police are doing an undercover operation. You're going to tell them that if they say anything to anyone, then you'll all go to prison for breaking and entering."

I don't like this. This is wrong. Policemen shouldn't do this. But if it is an undercover operation, then they don't want anyone to find out.

Robert takes over the talking now. "And nothing about this to your family, either. They don't need to worry about this. You wouldn't want to upset your mum, would you? Lovely lady," he says.

I don't like the way he says this. It sounds wrong. Robert is not a nice man. He was in my house this morning. He knows where I live, and I don't like it.

I nod my head.

Suddenly, Robert gets angry.

"You gone dumb, you little git?" he shouts. "Can't speak anymore?"

I'm scared now. Robert is not a nice man. I force myself to speak clearly.

"I understand," I say. "I won't tell anyone."

"And your friends," he says. "You'll make sure that they don't, as well. Because if they do, James, it'll be you we come to first. It'll be your house we come knocking at."

I nod. I look out of the window and I see Dave and Gilly. They're by the sycamore tree near Liv's house. Without realizing it, we've driven in a big circle. We are back near home.

"Stop the car," I say.

"What?" asks Robert.

"I can see my friends over there." I point to the tree.

Robert slows the car.

"So there they are. Little gits," says Simon. He takes the handcuffs off my wrists.

Robert stops the car just after the traffic lights. He turns round and looks into my eyes. I know now that he's not a good man. Before I thought he might be good. Now I know that he's not.

"Off you go, then, James. And don't forget what Simon says. Shtum." He makes a weird sound with his lips.

I get out of the car. I can feel Robert and Simon watching me. I want to run to the tree. To tell Gilly and Dave. I force myself to walk slowly.

I stop at the traffic lights to cross the road. I look left and the police car starts driving away. I walk across the road to where Dave and Gilly are standing under the tree.

"What was that?" asks Dave, when he sees me.

"Yeah, man, why didn't they arrest you?" asks Gilly.

"We didn't know what to do," says Dave. "We were going to tell your parents, but we didn't want us all to get into more trouble than we're already in."

Suddenly, I feel tired. I sigh deeply.

"What is it, Jay? What happened?" asks Dave.

Then I tell them everything that happened after they ran out of the house and left me with the weed plants. When I finish, they both look at me.

"Something's not right here," says Dave.

"What do you want to do?" asks Gilly.

"I don't know. I need to think about this," says Dave.

I don't want to think about it anymore. I just want to go home. I'm tired now. I want to go to bed. I want to sleep.

I can feel that something bad is going to happen. I don't know what it is. But it's going to be bad.

Chapter Eight

When I get home, Mum and Dad are in the lounge. They have the radio on. It smells of food in the house. Mum and Dad are sitting on the couch. They're looking through the old photo album.

"Hi, love," says Mum. "How's Dave?"

"He's good, thanks," I say. "What are you two doing?"

"Come and join us," says Dad. "Mum thinks it would be nice if we had any old photos of Mrs. Warren, to give them to her family."

"Why would we have photos of Mrs. Warren?" I ask.

"There was a big street party," says Mum. "Not long after we moved here. I think it was for the Queen's Golden Jubilee. You would have only been young. Not that you're old now." She laughs.

I think back. I do have a memory of the party. I remember tables and chairs in the street. Union Jack bunting hanging from the streetlights. Ham sandwiches. Cakes. Scones. I nod my head.

"Want to have a look with us?" asks Mum.

"OK," I say. I take my coat off and sit down on the couch in between Mum and Dad.

I look at the photos. There are lots of Mum and Dad when they were younger. Then there's *Nain* and *Taid*. And me.

There's a young me on a beach. The pictures don't look real. I wonder if that was me. I don't remember it. So how can it be me?

"Here they are," says Mum.

She places the big, green photo album on my lap. Mum and Dad both lean in closer to see the pictures.

There are nine pictures. I like this. They are taken in our street. They show people standing around talking. There's bunting hanging from the street lights. I can't recognise anyone.

"Turn over to the next page," Dad says. "I'm sure there was a big group photo. With everyone in it."

I turn the page. The photo album is heavy in my lap. There's a large group photo. There are about 20 people in the picture.

I don't count them. I'm trying not to count tonight. Tonight, there hasn't been much routine.

I look at the faces. I can see Mum and Dad. They look a lot younger. Dad's hair is longer. So is Mum's.

I can see Mrs. Warren. She looks the same. I can also see Mr. Edwards. He looks younger.

Why does Mrs. Warren look the same? Do you reach a certain age when you don't change anymore?

There's a young man standing next to Mr. Edwards. He looks familiar.

"Who's that?" I ask. I point my finger at the man standing next to Mr. Edwards.

"Oh, what's his name, Chris?" asks Mum. "Steven, is it?"

Dad leans in closer to look at the picture.

"Oh, you mean Mr. Edwards' adopted son? Simon, isn't it? A bad lad, he was," he says. "Got into trouble not long after this picture was taken. Went away after that. Don't think I've seen him since."

But I have.

I know who Simon is. I was sitting next to Simon earlier this evening. Simon is not a nice man. Simon is a bad policeman.

"Are you OK, Jay?" Dad asks.

"Yes," I answer. "I'm just tired. I think I'll go and get ready for bed."

"OK, love," Mum says and kisses me on the head. "Good night."

I get up from the couch. I give the photo album to Dad.

A plan is forming in my brain. I don't know the exact details yet. I need to lie down in my bed. I need to think clearly about the best thing to do. But first, I need my bedtime routine.

Chapter Nine

When the alarm clock goes off, I'm already awake.

I know what I'm going to do. I have a plan. I make sure my morning is as calm as possible. I need to be focused.

I get dressed. I have breakfast. I brush my teeth. I say goodbye to Mum. And I leave the house.

I do everything at the right time. I do everything the right number of times.

I walk to Dave's house. It's cold outside. The wind is blowing. The sky is grey. When I get to Dave's house, Dave and Gilly are waiting outside.

I don't like this. This is not part of my routine. I like Gilly. But Gilly doesn't come to Dave's house before school.

"Hi, Dave," I say. "Why are you here, Gilly?"

"Just a bit excited today," says Gilly.

"Why?" I ask.

"It's the school talent show," Gilly says. "This afternoon. In the hall, at two o'clock. Had you forgotten?"

I had forgotten. I'd been thinking about Mrs. Warren too much. And the policemen. And what I wanted to do today.

"Sorry, Gil," I say. "I had forgotten. I'm really looking forward to it now, though. Your moves are ace. I want to see Liv play the guitar again, too."

"Me too," says Dave.

"Guys," I say. "I found something out last night."

I tell Dave and Gilly about the photo album. Then I tell them about my plan.

The school day passes slowly. I can't concentrate in lessons. I keep thinking about after school. I don't know if I'm doing the right thing. Dave and Gilly thought I was right, though.

Liv doesn't look well in class. She looks pale and sick. I hope she does play the guitar and sing.

Gilly is excited all day. He's going to perform an acrobat routine on stage. He's going to walk on his hands. He's going to do cartwheels. And backflips. And hang upside down from ropes.

It's going to be good.

Chapter Ten

After school, I feel strange.

Liv didn't play the guitar and sing. She didn't go onto the stage.

Gilly went on the stage. So did eight other children. Some sang. Some danced. One boy kicked a football in the air 124 times without it touching the floor.

After school, there was an ambulance in the playground. I think they took Liv to the hospital. I hope she's OK. When I see her, I want to talk to her. I don't know what I'll say.

I meet Dave and Gilly outside the school. They want to walk with me to the police station. This is not part of my plan. I'm happy to have them with me, though.

It takes 21 minutes to walk to the police station. I feel nervous when we get there. I stop and look at Dave and Gilly.

"You sure you want to do this on your own?" Dave asks.

I nod.

"We'll be right here waiting the whole time," says Gilly.

"And if you're more than half an hour, we're coming in to find you," says Dave.

"OK," I say.

I walk into the police station.

Inside, there's a reception desk. A lady is sitting on a chair behind the desk. There are no other people in there. It is very warm. I unzip my coat. I walk to the desk.

"Hello," the lady says. "How can I help you, young man?"

"I'd like to report a crime," I say.

"OK, if you'd like to take a seat, I'll see if one of our officers is available," she says.

The lady stands up. She's not very tall. She wears glasses and has dark brown hair. She looks kind.

I hope she doesn't find Robert or Simon. That would not be good.

I sit down on a plastic chair. It's like the ones in school. It's not comfortable. The lady opens a door behind her and goes out of the room.

I wait for three minutes. The lady comes back into the room from the same door. A policewoman comes into the reception area through a different door to my right. She smiles at me. She looks kind.

"Hello," she says. "I'm PC Johnson. Would you like to come with me?"

We go into a different room. This room is smaller. There's a table with four chairs. Two on either side.

"Take a seat," the police lady says.

I sit down. She sits down opposite me.

"Before we start, I need to know your age," she says.

"I'm 13," I tell her.

"OK. This means that I can't take a formal statement from you without an adult present. Do you still want to tell me about this crime you witnessed?" she asks.

I think for a moment. Then I decide to continue. I'm here now. I didn't like coming here. It definitely wasn't part of any routine.

"Yes, please," I say.

"OK, let's make a start," she says.

She takes out a notebook and pen. She asks me my name. She writes it down. And my address.

"OK, James," she says. "Where do you want to start?"

I tell her about the incident at Mrs. Warren's house. I tell her how Mr. Edwards knew Mrs. Warren and told Mum about the burglary. I tell her about the policeman coming to our house.

When I say his name is Robert, her face changes slightly. She doesn't think I saw it. But I did.

Then I tell her about the van. Ford Transit LT56 YTJ. I tell her about Dave and Gilly. I tell her about our plan. Then I tell her what we saw in the loft room of the rented house.

I tell her what happened with the two policemen. I tell her how they drove me round. How they told me they were working on an undercover operation. And I couldn't tell anyone.

Then I tell her how I saw Simon. The policeman. In the photo with Mr. Edwards and Mrs. Warren. I tell her how Dad said that Simon was Mr. Edwards' adopted son. How he was bad and went away.

Then I tell her some things that I haven't told anyone else. Some things I've been thinking about. Some things that made me want to come here today. Some things I haven't even told to Dave and Gilly.

I tell her how I'd seen the two plumbers in the street. I tell her that they were wearing baseball caps. I tell her that they looked down when I was near them. I tell her that I was 97% sure that the plumbers were Robert and Simon.

I tell her that I notice things about people. About the way they move. The way they walk.

I tell her that I heard them speaking. The plumbers. They were speaking in a foreign accent. I thought it was Polish.

But then I thought, *Why would they speak to each other in English?*

I see people all the time from different places. They always talk to each other in their own language.

Then I thought about the plumbers. The way they spoke. The way they moved. And I knew that they weren't foreign. I knew that they were pretending to be.

Then I tell her the last thing I want to say. The most important thing. I tell her about Mr. Edwards. I tell her how I'd seen him speaking to the men with the baseball caps. Outside the rented house.

I tell her how he'd looked angry. I tell her how he'd shouted at the men. I tell her what I heard him say: "You better not mess this up. I've got a lot of fingers in a lot of pies. And I don't want you two idiots messing it all up for me."

I tell her how I thought it was a strange thing to say. Why would Mr. Edwards have his fingers in pies? Was he testing them to see if they were hot enough? And what did it have to do with the plumbers?

Then I tell her that afterward I thought about the pies. I knew it meant something else. I remembered this once I'd started thinking about the incident at Mrs. Warren's house. After we went into the rented house.

Finally, I tell her that I'm sorry.

"I'm sorry about going into that house," I say. 'We just wanted to find out what happened to Mrs. Warren. It was because of what the policeman said. Robert. When he came to our house. About something out of the ordinary. That's where it started. That's what made me think of these things. Because I knew that it wasn't a coincidence. I don't think it's a coincidence. Do you?"

I finish speaking. The police lady carries on writing for nearly a minute. Then she stops. She looks me in the eye. She looks happy.

"Is this all the truth, James?" she asks.

I nod.

"I don't like lies," I say.

"Neither do I," she says. "And no, I don't think that any of this is coincidental at all."

I have never heard the word coincidental before. It sounds like it would be hard to say. I know, though, that it means coincidence.

"OK, James. You've been really helpful today," she says. "I'm so glad you came in. This has been very interesting. I can't say any more at the moment. But would you be willing to come back to the station with one of your parents to make a formal statement? If we need you to."

"Yes," I say.

"Thank you," she says. "I really do appreciate what you've done today. It must have taken a lot. You're a very brave young man."

I smile.

She takes me back to the reception. I say goodbye to the police lady and the reception lady. The police lady thanks me again and I go outside.

It's very cold outside now. It's darker, too. It's not completely dark. I look at my watch. I've been in the police station for 20 minutes.

I look around to find Dave and Gilly. I can't see them.

I walk across the car park. There are benches on the street outside the car park. I can see the back of Dave's head now. It's moving left and right. He must be speaking to Gilly.

Suddenly, I hear a shout.

"Oy, you!"

I turn to look. My heart feels like it jumps into my throat.

It's Simon. He's seen me. He starts walking quickly toward me.

I start walking faster. I turn to look, and he's running now.

"Oy, you! Stop there. I need to talk to you," he shouts.

I start running.

"Dave! Gilly!" I shout.

Dave turns round. He can see me running. So can Gilly. They look confused. Then they see Simon. They understand. They get up and start running, too.

I'm running as fast as I can now. Dave and Gilly are about 100 metres ahead of me. I look backwards and I'm shocked. Simon is right there. He's caught up to me very quickly.

He reaches out. His fingers grab my coat. I shake my sleeves free and let him pull my jacket away from me. He throws it to the ground. He keeps running. He's about to grab me again.

There's no time. He's too fast.

I turn suddenly and run across the road.

I hear the screech of brakes. I hear a shout from the pavement. Then I feel the car hit me in the side.

For a second, I don't feel anything. Time seems like it has stopped.

I can see the dull, grey sky. I can see the green of the trees on the other side of the road. Then my head hits the pavement and everything goes black.

Chapter Eleven

I open my eyes. I don't know where I am. My head hurts.

I look round. I'm lying on a bed. There's a curtain around the bed. It looks like a shower curtain. I can hear noises from behind the curtain.

I think I'm in the hospital.

Then I remember. The police station. Being chased. Losing my coat. Running into the road.

Then, bang. The feel of hard metal. The feel of hard tarmac on my head. Then, nothing.

No wonder my head hurts.

I think about what happened. I think about Dave and Gilly. Are they here? Did Simon chase them after I was hit by the car? Do Mum and Dad know? Are they here?

I see the curtain start to move. It starts sliding back. A nurse stands there. She smiles at me. She has very white skin and red lips. She reminds me of Liv.

"Hello," she says. "You've had quite an exciting day, I hear."

Where did she hear that? I think.

"I'm Caroline. I've just come to do your obs. To see how you are. Is that OK?" she asks.

I nod. I don't know what obs are. I don't ask her.

She holds a clipboard with paper attached. She looks at it. Then she puts it down on a tray at the bottom of the bed.

"Have you ever had your blood pressure taken before, James?"

she asks.

"Yes," I say.

A doctor took my blood pressure once. The doctor who gave me the tablets that made me feel sick. I felt like my arm was going to explode. It didn't hurt. I didn't like it or not like it. It was OK.

The nurse takes my blood pressure. Then she puts a thermometer in my mouth. I have to lift up my tongue. This is to see how hot or cold I am. I don't feel hot or cold.

The nurse takes the thermometer out of my mouth. She writes on the paper on the clipboard.

"OK, James. All looks good here," she says. "How's your head? Does it hurt?"

"A little bit," I say.

"Do you want anything for the pain?" she asks.

I look at her. I think she means medicine. I shake my head.

"Are you sure?" she asks.

"Yes, thank you," I say.

"I've got a couple of people here who'd really like to see you," she says. "Do you think that you're ready for some visitors?"

"Yes," I say. "Who is it?"

She smiles.

"I'll be back in a sec," she says.

A sec is short for a second. I like this. A min is short for a minute, but you don't say min. You can write min or mins, but not say it. You can say "back in a sec" but not "back in a min."

The nurse goes away. She leaves the curtain slightly open. I look past the open part of the curtain. A doctor or nurse walks past. I don't know which.

Then a man pushes a stretcher past with a person lying on it. I think about Mrs. Warren. I think about what's happened. I hope that the police will do something about Simon and Robert.

The nurse comes back. She looks worried. She opens the curtain wider. Robert is standing behind her. He's wearing his police uniform.

I panic.

I try to get up. I slide out of the bed. My head feels strange. It hurts. I feel dizzy.

"It's OK," says the nurse. 'This policeman has some news for you. Some news you're going to want to hear."

But I'm not listening. I've pulled the curtains back on the other side of the bed. I pull them back and move away from the bed. But then I walk into another bed.

A boy looks up at me. He is shocked. He doesn't look well.

"James," I hear the nurse say.

I open the curtain at the end of the boy's bed. I walk quickly away from his bed. It all looks the same. I don't know which way to go.

Then Robert appears in front of me.

"James, please. This is not what you think," he says.

Then I see Mum and Dad behind him. And Dave and Gilly. What's going on? I don't know what to do.

Mum comes toward me. She hugs me. She looks like she's been crying. Dad comes over, too.

"I'm sorry, Jay," she says. "We just thought you'd want to know as soon as possible. We had no idea what you'd done. All three of you. You've been so brave."

I go back to my bed. I sit up with my legs stretched out. I feel weak. I feel dizzy. But I feel OK now.

I know that Mum and Dad are here. And Dave and Gilly. They came over, too. They both hugged me. They've never done that before. It was strange. It was nice.

Mum and Dad tell me to listen to Robert. They would come back soon. Robert sits on a chair next to my bed. He tells me what happened.

Robert is an undercover policeman. Simon is a policeman. Simon is also Mr. Edwards' adopted son. Nobody knew Simon was Mr. Edwards' son until I told the police lady.

Robert has been investigating Simon. Simon is corrupt. Like the Nigerian government. And the UK government. Robert has pretended to be corrupt, too. So he can find out what Simon is doing.

Simon is growing weed in the rented house. Simon burgled Mrs. Warren's house because he knew she had lots of valuable jewelry. He knew this because Mr. Edwards knew this. The police didn't know this.

The police knew that Simon was working for someone. Someone higher up. A bigger criminal. They didn't know who.

Now, they do. It's Mr. Edwards.

Simon owed Mr. Edwards lots of money. Mr. Edwards made

Simon do things to pay back the money. He made him join the police so he could find things out. Mr. Edwards wanted to know about what the police were doing. It made it easier for him to commit crime.

Simon has admitted everything. Mr. Edwards has been arrested. He was very angry. He shouted at Robert. He didn't see Simon.

Mr. Edwards did lots of bad things. He organised where the weed was sold. He arranged for it to be given to different criminals all over the city.

He also made Simon tell him about empty houses. Mr. Edwards bought these houses. Mr. Edwards bought the rented house we went into. Mr. Edwards used a different name to buy the houses. He used a holding company.

Mr. Edwards used the houses for crime. He grew weed in some houses. He used others as brothels. A brothel is a bad place. This is what Robert says. He tells me it's where girls are forced to do things they don't want to.

Mr. Edwards also used the houses to watch other houses. People who work for Mr. Edwards, like Simon, watch other people's houses from the houses Mr. Edwards owns. They see where old people live alone. Then they tell Mr. Edwards. Then someone else burgles the house.

Mr. Edwards has done lots of bad things. He is a hardened criminal. This is what Robert says. Hardened means that he's worse than other criminals.

I didn't know there were different types of criminals.

I never liked Mr. Edwards. But I thought he was just a grumpy old codger.

Chapter Twelve

Robert has gone. I'm on my own. Mum and Dad have been back to see me. So have Dave and Gilly.

They all had lots to say to me. About Mr. Edwards. About the police. About going into the rented house.

I didn't have a lot to say to them. I feel tired now.

Mum and Dad and Dave and Gilly have gone home now. They are coming back in the morning. The nurse tells me that I can go home in the morning.

I have to stay in the hospital overnight. This is so they know I don't have concussion. Concussion is a serious head injury. I don't think I have concussion. My head still hurts. Not as much, though.

A nurse comes to see me every hour. She does my obs. At first, it was Caroline. Now, it's a different nurse.

This nurse is smaller. Her name is Agila. She's from the Philippines. She asks me what school I go to. I tell her. She tells me that her daughter goes to the same school. Her daughter is in my class. Her name is Diwa.

Agila is nice. She is gentle. I ask her what obs means. It means observations. It is shortened. I like this.

I am allowed to walk around the ward. There are lots of children here. Some are very ill. Some have broken legs. Some are recovering from operations.

I smile at the other children. Some smile back. Some don't. I'm walking past a hospital bed and I hear someone speak.

"Hey, Jay."

I think I've heard it wrong, at first. I look round. I haven't heard it wrong.

It's Liv.

Liv from school is lying in a hospital bed. She looks very ill. She has a tube going into her arm. This is called a drip. The nurse told me it's to give medicine or water straight into your blood. I like this. This is good.

Liv moves her arm. She beckons me to come closer. I walk over to her bed.

"Hey, Jay," she says again.

She always says "hey" instead of "hi" or "hello." I like it.

"Hi, Liv," I say.

Usually, I feel nervous speaking to girls. I don't feel nervous now.

"What are you doing in here?" she asks me.

"I got hit by a car," I tell her.

"Wow, are you OK?" she asks.

"I cut my head on the road. I need to stay in hospital overnight. For obs," I say.

"Obvs," she says, and laughs. This is a joke, but I don't understand it.

"Why are you in here, Liv?' I ask her. "Is that water in the drip, or medicine?"

"It's antibiotics," she says.

"Are you ill?" I ask.

"I was. I'm getting better now," she says. "I did something really stupid, but now I'm OK. I'm going to get better. And I'm going to talk to Mum more."

Liv looks scared. She's pretending to be OK, but I can tell she's not.

"It's good to talk to your mum," I say. "I talk to mine sometimes. About things that happen. Things that I think about. Not everything."

"God, no," she says. "Imagine that."

She laughs again.

"Hey, Jay, can I ask you something?" she asks.

"Yes," I say.

"How come you never speak to me in school?" she asks.

I think about this for a minute. I know it's because I'm nervous. Because I can't speak to girls. Only Mum. But it's also because I like Liv.

This makes me feel strange. I don't want to tell her. But I don't want to lie.

"I just feel nervous talking to girls," I say. "Especially pretty ones."

She laughs. Then she smiles.

"Will you promise me something, Jay?" she asks.

"OK," I say. *It depends what it is,* I think.

"When we're both out of here. When we're back in school. Promise me that you'll talk to me," she says. "That you'll come and sit with me like this. You see, you've done it now, so you know there's nothing to be nervous about."

I think about this.

"OK," I say. "I promise. But it is different in school."

"What do you mean?" she asks.

"It's a different place," I say. "There are lots of people everywhere. It's very loud. I sometimes feel nervous in school even when I'm not speaking to a girl."

"That's OK. As long as you try. I'll try, too. Do you think that we could be friends, Jay? I could do with a friend right now," she says.

"Yes," I say. "Definitely."

She smiles again. She has a pretty face. I haven't seen her smile before. When she smiles, her eyes crinkle at the corners and go shiny. It's nice.

I like Liv. She's my friend row. Like Dave and Gilly. But different.

I know Dave and Gilly better. But now that I've spoken to Liv, I feel like I could speak to her forever. That I could tell her anything. More than I could ever tell Mum or Dad or Dave or Gilly.

"Do you want to hear a story?" I ask her.

She smiles again. I like it.

"Yes, please," she says.

I start at the start.

"I hear the noises in the street before I see what's happening. Loud sirens. Shouting. I feel my heart beating faster in my chest. This is not good," I say.

Then I tell her about everything that's happened over the last few days.

She listens. She doesn't speak. She watches my face as I talk.

When I reach the end, I finish by telling her how I was walking round the hospital and I heard someone say, "Hey, Jay."

Then I say, "And you know the story from there. Because that's the part that you're in."

"I was in it a little bit earlier on, too," she says.

She smiles. I smile.

"Thank you, Jay," she says. "That was the best story anyone's ever told me."

www.ingramcontent.com/pod-product-compliance
Lightning Source LLC
Chambersburg PA
CBHW072233190626
46809CB00017B/1921